LEVEL 1 Reader

DreamWorks GABBY'S DOLLHOUSE

SLEEPOVER PARTY

Adapted by **GABRIELLE REYES**

SCHOLASTIC INC.

ISBN 978-1-338-88541-5

10 9 8 7 6   24 25 26 27

Printed in the U.S.A.   40

First printing 2023

Book design by **SALENA MAHINA** and **STACIE ZUCKER**

FREE DOWNLOAD
TÉLÉCHARGEMENT GRATUIT

Download on the
App Store

GET IT ON
Google Play

Télécharger dans l'App Store
Disponible sur Google Play

GabbysDollhouse.spinmaster.com

Kitty Fairy is having a sleepover.

Pandy Paws and I are so excited!

1

We ask Pillow Cat to join us.

Pillow Cat is nervous.

She has never been to a sleepover.

This is my first sleepover, too.

We can do it together!

Pillow Cat wants to try.

Let's give it a go!

First, we need pajamas.

Kitty Fairy leads the way.

I pick a top from the pajama tree.

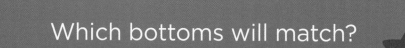

Which bottoms will match?

These PJs are paw-some!

It is Pandy's turn!

Pandy picks pants.

Which top will match?

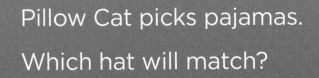

Pillow Cat picks pajamas.

Which hat will match?

We look purr-rific, don't you think?

Kitty Fairy says we need one more thing.

Kitty Fairy uses her garden magic.

Pillow Cat gets fairy wings!

Her wings are dreamy.

Pandy gets fairy wings.

His wings are sparkly.

I get fairy wings, too.

My wings are a-meow-zing!

We fly to Fizzy Juice Falls.

It is our first time flying.

Flying is fun!

We try fizzy juice for the first time.

It is yummy!

Then we try rainbow fairy popcorn.

What a tasty snack!

Next, we brush our teeth.

The toothbrushes have wings, too!

It is getting dark.

We lie on our sleeping bags and look at the starry sky.

We look for shapes.

I see Pandy!

Pandy sees a surfboard!

Do you see a surfboard?

Pillow Cat sees a big pillow.

Do you see a big pillow?

Pillow Cat has an idea!

She tells us a starry bedtime story.

Once upon a time . . .

Pandy surfed the stars.

He surfed all over the night sky.

Then he fell asleep.

He had sweet dreams of hot dogs and pickles!

Great story, Pillow Cat!

We see something else in the stars!

Flower fireworks!

It's garden magic!

28

Pillow Cat is so happy she came.

Our first sleepover is meow-mazing!

Thank you for trying new things with us!

What is something you want to try?

Give it a go!